My Friend Ben and the Big Race

Charles Beyl

Albert Whitman & Company
Chicago, Illinois

To Sue and Elizabeth for believing in Chip and Ben as much as I do.

Library of Congress Cataloging-in-Publication data is on file with the publisher.

Text and illustrations copyright © 2022 by Charles Beyl
First published in the United States of America in 2022 by Albert Whitman & Company

ISBN 978-0-8075-5464-7 (hardcover)
ISBN 978-0-8075-5467-8 (ebook)

Printed in China
10 9 8 7 6 5 4 3 2 1 WKT 26 25 24 23 22 21

Design by Aphelandra

For more information about Albert Whitman & Company,
visit our website at www.albertwhitman.com.

I'm Chip and this is my friend Ben.
We love to swim.

At my house, we swim to Turtle's Cove and Rainbow Falls.

At Ben's house, we see how deep we can dive near Big Rocks.

We are hungry after we swim.

We eat Mom's twig-and-maple-leaf sandwiches.

They taste really good.

When we swim at my house, we see Catfish in his cave.

We always say, "Hello, Catfish."

He always makes funny fish sounds.

FLUBBLUBBUB

Today he says, "You beaver boys are good swimmers! Do you think you can swim as fast as me?"

"Maybe," Ben and I both say.

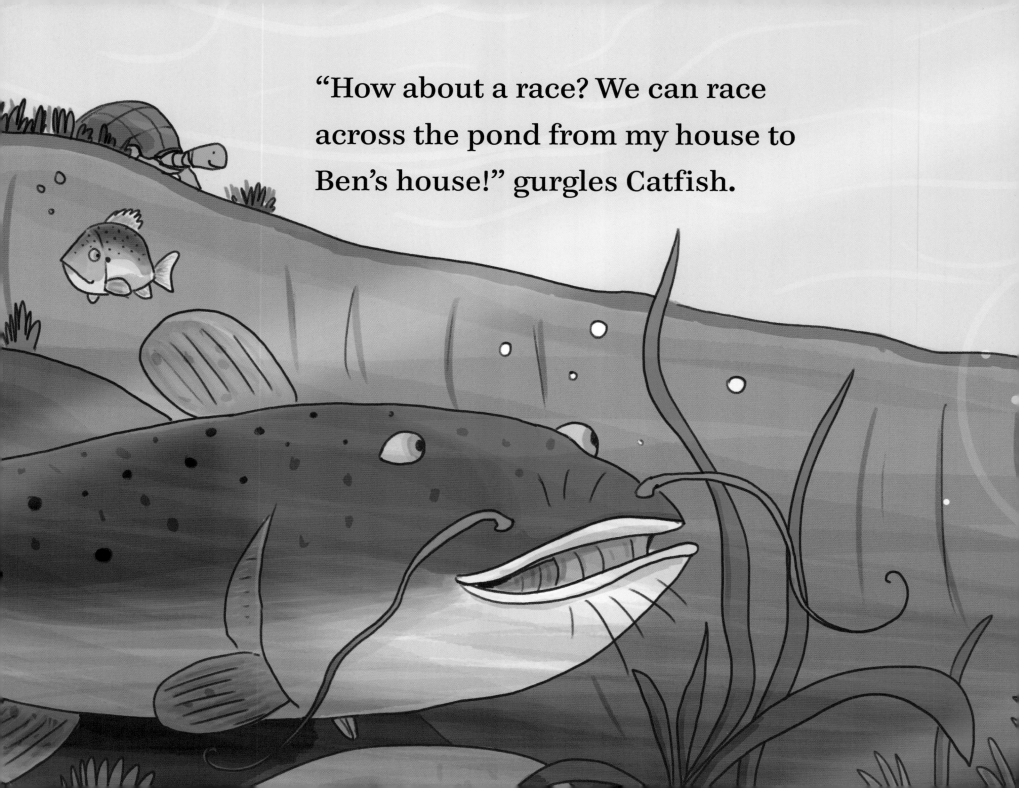

"How about a race? We can race across the pond from my house to Ben's house!" gurgles Catfish.

"Okay! But we have to ask our parents first," we tell Catfish.

Our parents
say it's okay.
They'll meet us
at the finish line
at Ben's house.
Mom promises to
bring sandwiches.

Ben and I have never
swum all the way
across the pond.
It looks like a long
way. Ben says, "It will
be an adventure!"

Turtle wants to race too!

I like when Turtle swims with us.

He knows all the best rocks to sit on.

Ben is ready. I am ready. Turtle is ready.

"Go!" shouts Catfish.

We swim fast, paddling with our legs and steering with our tails. Catfish swims like a streak of lightning. Swimming fast is fun! Turtle is right behind us.

Catfish burbles back to us,

"Don't wiggle! Paddle! Go faster!"

I pop my head out of the water.
There's Rainbow Falls! It looks pretty.

"Get back under! Keep swimming!" gurgles Catfish.

"You can't win if you are sightseeing!

Catfish is in the lead.

Ben is in second place and swimming very fast.

I hope he waits for me.

I am getting tired.

Turtle asks, "Do you want to rest?
I know a good rock that
we can sit on."

It feels good to rest.

I wish I had one of Mom's sandwiches.

I wish I were pretending and exploring with Ben.

This isn't fun anymore.

"Come on!"
I tell Turtle.
"Let's finish!"

Halfway across the pond, I pop up.

Ben is waiting for me!

"I missed you! Do you want to play deep-sea divers instead?" Ben asks.

"Let's finish and then play!" I answer.

Now, Ben and I paddle faster than ever, so we can play.

Our parents cheer, "Ben, Chip, and Turtle swam all the way across the pond!"

Catfish makes funny fish noises and goes back to his cave.

The twig-and-maple-leaf sandwiches Mom brought look better than ever.

Ben and I play deep-sea divers
the rest of the day.

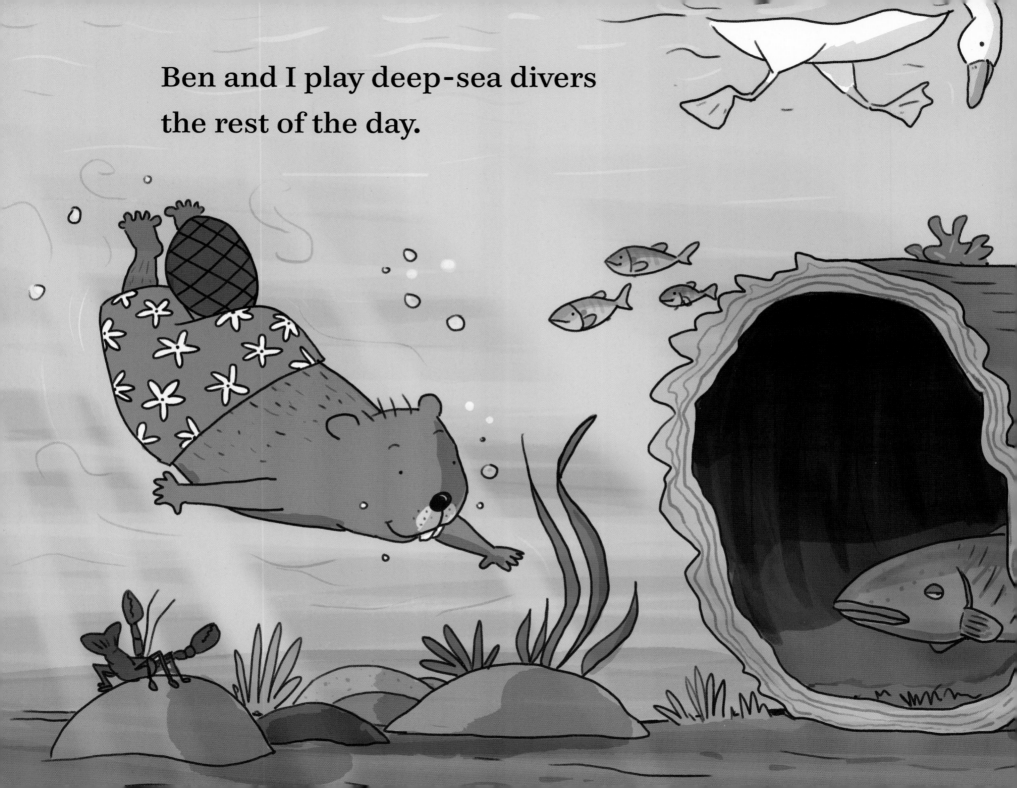

It's good to know we can swim
all the way across the pond,
but Ben and I like being explorers.

Maybe Turtle will play with us tomorrow.